W9-BRJ-530

The Llamacorn is Kind

By Kate Coombs

Art by

Elisa Pallmer

The Llamacorn is Kind

By Kate Coombs

Art by

Elisa Pallmer

GIBBS SMITH
TO ENRICH AND INSPIRE HUMANKIND

The **unicorn** is pale and grand.
She paces gravely through the land.

But the **llamacorn** is kind.

The **girafficorn** has his head in the clouds.

The **donkeycorn**
is loud, loud, loud!

But the **llamacorn** is kind.

The **buffalocorn**
bumps into you.

The **COWICORN**
has a mournful moo.

The **walruscorn**
is large and blue.

But the **llamacorn** is kind.

The **goaticorn** eats everything.

The **gorillacorn** is sad.

The **snakicorn's** busy
with loop-di-loops,

and the camelcorn's always mad.

You don't want to bother
the **bearicorn**—

He pops
the birthday balloons
with his horn.

The **flamingocorn** dances,
she twirls and sings.

She uses her horn
to juggle things.

She's fun to know.
She can put on a show—

but the **llamacorn** is kind.

The **tigercorn** walks with a fearsome tread.
His horn is enormous and heavy as lead.

The **mousicorn's** silly.
She jumps on the bed.

But the **llamacorn** is kind.

Oh the one-horned beasts are a magical crowd,

sad or happy, quiet or loud,

big or little, shy or proud—

but watch for the one
who will be your friend,

who will share
his cookies

and play pretend,

the nicest creature
you'll ever find—

the **llamacorn** is kind.

Manufactured in Guangdong, China, in May 2019 by RR Donnelley

First Edition

23 22 21 20 19   5 4 3 2 1

Published by
Gibbs Smith
P.O. Box 667
Layton, Utah 84041
1.800.835.4993 orders
www.gibbs-smith.com

Designed by Elisa Pallmer

Gibbs Smith books are printed on either recycled, 100% post-consumer waste,
FSC-certified papers or on paper produced from sustainable PEFC-certified forest/controlled wood source.
Learn more at www.pefc.org.

Library of Congress Control Number: 2018968460
ISBN: 978-1-4236-5262-5